This book belongs to

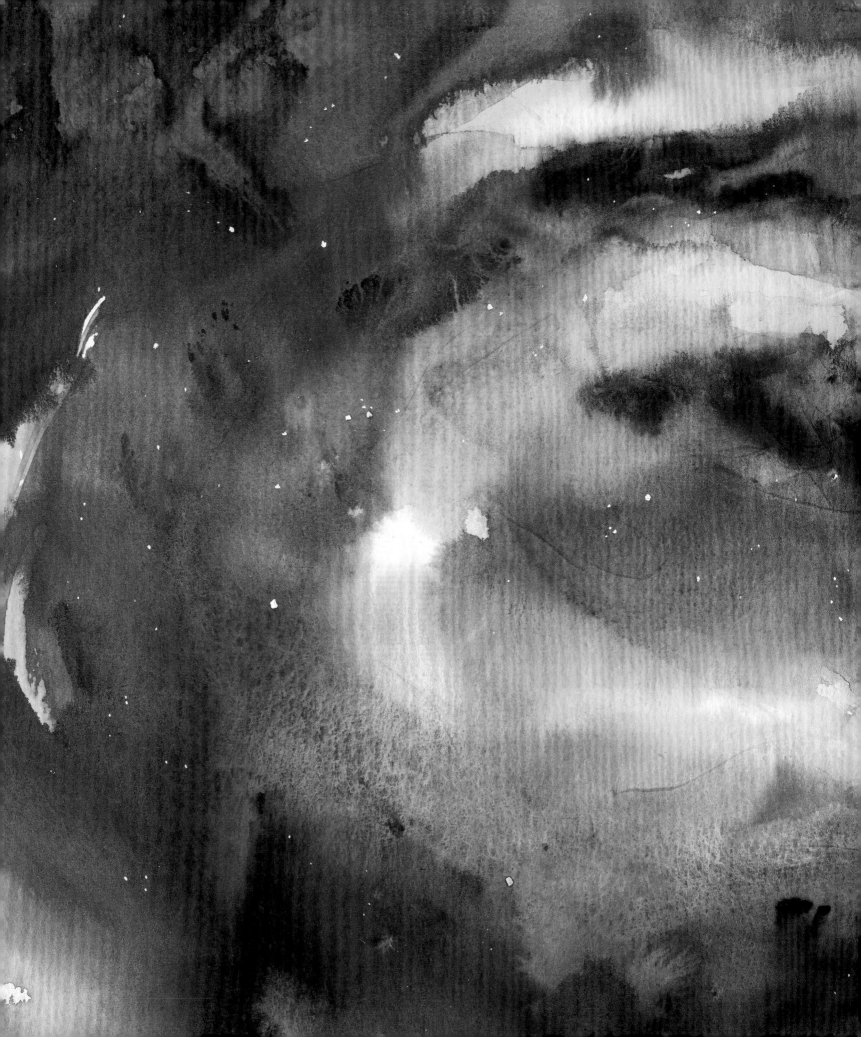

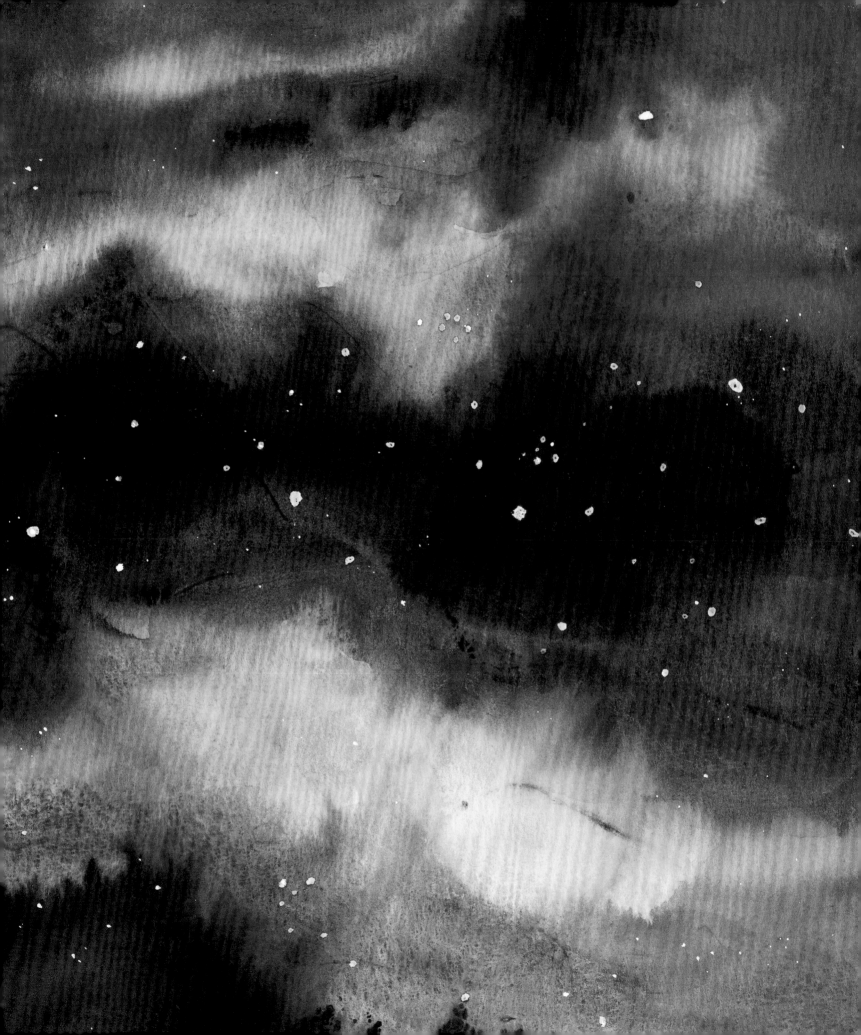

For Richard, Frances, Rachel, Joseph, Theo, Araba, Tom, Jenny, Ana and Jack
G.L.

For all my Family in Germany
(Für meine ganze Familie in Deutschland)
K.L.

First published in Great Britain in 2009 by Gullane Children's Books
This paperback edition published 2010 by
Gullane Children's Books
185 Fleet Street, London, EC4A 2HS
www.gullanebooks.com

1 3 5 7 9 10 8 6 4 2

Text © Gillian Lobel 2009   Illustrations © Karin Littlewood 2009

The right of Gillian Lobel and Karin Littlewood to be identified as the author and illustrator of this work
has been asserted by them in accordance with the Copyright, Designs and Patents Act, 1988.
A CIP record for this title is available from the British Library.

ISBN: 978-1-86233-782-4

Printed and bound in China

Moonshadow

Gillian Lobel

illustrated by Karin Littlewood

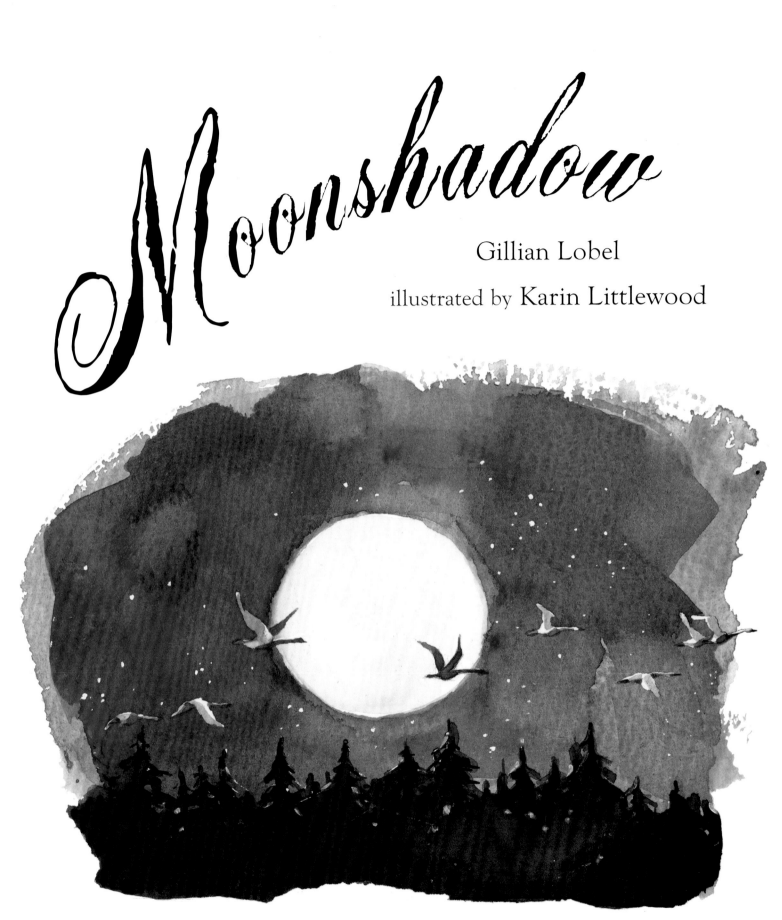

GULLANE
CHILDREN'S BOOKS

High above the earth flew the swans. White wings
feathered the wind, and the air was loud with their joyful cries.
"Going South!" they said. "To the warm sun and the green fields."
Moonshadow shivered with excitement as he watched,
snuggled up close to his grandfather.

"When are *we* going, Grandfather?" he asked.
"Very soon, Moonshadow!" said Grandfather.
"But *where* are we all going?"
"To the warm lands, Little One; it is
much too cold for us here, in the winter."
"Will I – will I be able to fly that far?"

"Yes, my Little One. I will lead you,
by sun and stars, as my father did before me."
Gently Grandfather nibbled Moonshadow's feathers. And
Moonshadow knew that everything would be all right.

Suddenly, from the North, a fierce, cold wind blew.
The flock stirred, beating their wings, and straining their necks.
"Now!" cried Grandfather. "The time is right!" And he began the
strong, slow run to take off, his wings beating the air.
Moonshadow ran like the wind . . .

And then he was up, up and away, high in
the blue, leaving the icy marshes below him.

He flew close to his mother and father, lifted on the strong upbeat of the circling wings. All through the night they flew, pale shadows in the moonlight, over the cold brown lands, through the stinging snowflakes, on, on never stopping.

Sunrise washed their feathers with gold and rose, and still
they flew, over the sleeping towns, over rooftops and domes,
until the land slipped away, and they came to the wrinkled sea.

The little swan beat his wings fiercely, trying so hard not to slip behind. A burning ache filled his body. Grandfather knew that his little ones were weary. Whooping loudly, he spiralled downwards to a tiny island.

Moonshadow sighed with relief. How good it was to slide along the water, and furl his wings! He gazed up at the stars blazing overhead. And then he saw a wonder . . .

The sky was lit by sheets of swirling lights.
"Whatever is it, Father?" cried Moonshadow.
"The Dancing Lights of the North," said Father. "They shine for us!"
"Now sleep," said Mother. "You have a long journey ahead."
Moonshadow watched until his eyelids drooped, and he fell
into a deep sleep. But Grandfather stayed awake, guarding his flock.

At sunrise, they were off again. Moonshadow felt new strength flow into his wings. That day, the flying was easy. But when night came, the air froze, and the stars disappeared. How would Grandfather guide them now?

The wind grew fierce, and lightning ripped the clouds. For a second the whole flock glowed white. Then the sky roared, and hard balls of ice beat against Moonshadow's head. He could no longer hear the beat of his parents' wings.

"Mother! Father!"
he cried in terror.
"Where are you?"
He started to fall,
spinning down, down.

And then he felt strong wings beneath
him and knew that his mother and father
were there, drawing him on with the power
of their wings and the strength of their love.

Slowly the wind dropped, and the air softened. They saw
land, and flew down to rest. Moonshadow looked all around.
"Mother!" he gasped. "I can't see Grandfather!"
"He fell in the storm," said his mother sadly.

Moonshadow's heart overflowed with sorrow.
"Who will lead us now, Father?" he cried.
"I will," said his father. "Follow me, my son.
We must go on, even though our hearts are heavy."

Over the purple moors they flew, over green hills and
chequered fields. And just as the sun was setting, and
Moonshadow felt he could go on no longer, they
came to a place of great shining waters.

Moonshadow's father began a slow, wide circle, then started the final slide to the silver lake. Suddenly Moonshadow was down too. The whole flock were whooping and bobbing their necks with joy. Moonshadow dipped his beak into the water and sipped the rich, good food.

Great trees fringed the lake, glowing amber and gold.
He fluffed out his feathers. All around him, his family
glided over the lake. No – not all his family:

Grandfather was not there.
Moonshadow's heart ached and he hung his head.

His father caressed him gently.
"Grandfather will always be in our hearts, where
nothing can take him from us, Moonshadow. And the flock
will go on. I will lead now – as one day you will, my son."

Moonshadow looked proudly at his father.
Then, safe and warm, in the heart of his family,
he tucked his head under his wing, and slept.

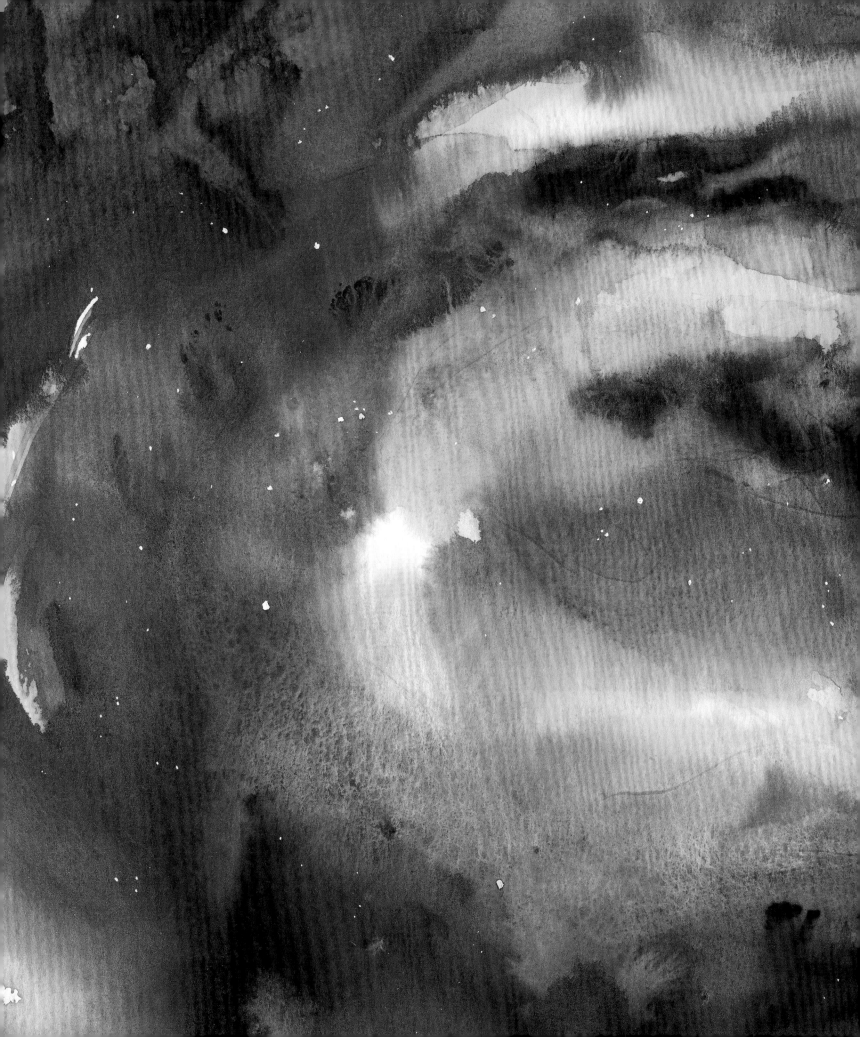

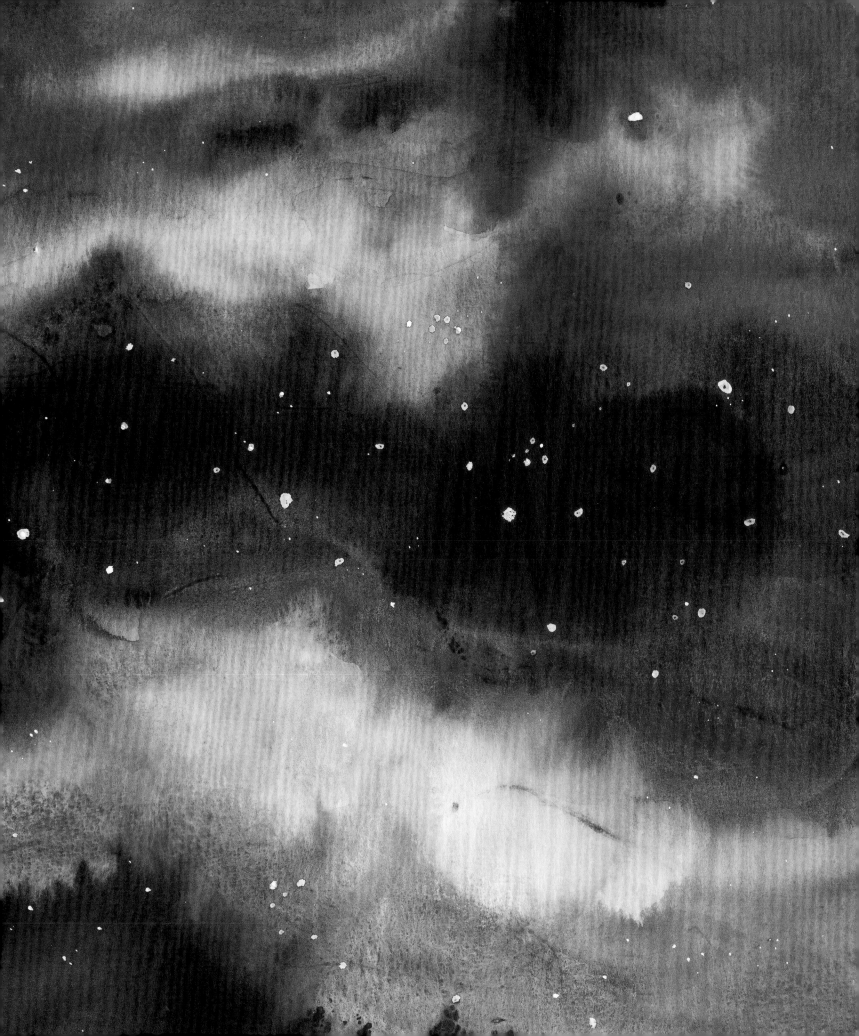

Other books by Karin Littlewood

Immi

One day, Immi finds a colourful wooden bird at the end of her fishing line. The next day she finds a red flower, followed by an orange starfish. But where do these bright gifts come from? And who can Immi thank for the joy they have given her?

The Most Important Gift of All
WRITTEN BY DAVID CONWAY

What gift should Ama give her new baby brother to welcome him into the world? The gift of *love*, Grandma Sisi tells her. But where can Ama find this precious gift?

Other books by Gillian Lobel

For Everyone to Share
ILLUSTRATED BY DANIEL HOWARTH

Little Mouse has never been out of his nest before and he is thrilled by the sights and sounds outside. But what is this amazing place – and who is it for?